PRAISE FOR THE UNBEARABLE TASTE OF FRUIT AND WINE

"In this beautiful tale of Iris, isolated with her so called family that only wants to use her, RSA Garcia skillfully illustrates that not all cages are physical . . . and there are some only we have the ability to free ourselves from. Beautifully written. Intensely emotional. Powerful."
—Jodi Meadows, *New York Times* bestselling author

"The truths Iris knows protect her, and everyone around her. But these truths hide a secret - one that those she loves best will do anything to keep from her. In RSA Garcia's richly imagined world of mages, monsters, and thieves, Iris' transformation is nothing short of world shaking. An excellent adventure."
—Fran Wilde, two-time Nebula award winning author

"*The Unbearable Taste of Fruit and Wine* is a lush, beautifully written novella filled with intrigue and romance. R.S.A. Garcia has a gift for subtle language, effortlessly weaving complex characters into a beautiful, mysterious world."
—Amy James, author of *A Five Letter Word for Love*

THE UNBEARABLE TASTE OF FRUIT AND WINE

R.S.A. GARCIA

CONTENTS

1

— · —

THE MAGUS OF THE VALE'S VAULT

The soft, ever-shifting glow of the rainbow path at Iris's feet wound through the cluttered room toward the back wall. Rubbing her arms for warmth under her cloak, she followed it, edging around statues and paintings, cabinets and shelves, shapes covered with cloth, and bags spilling their contents onto the floor. This was one of the largest collections of artefacts she'd ever seen—aside from father's—and she took her time as she moved through it, letting the moonlight streaming in through the one small, high window be her guide.

The rainbow ended at the base of a dusty trunk and faded away as she stopped in front of it. Iris crouched to remove the vases and bowls of jewels atop it, surprised to see it was unlocked. Inside, a red velvet cloth pockmarked with insect holes lay over the contents. She unfolded it and hesitated a second, staring down at what lay inside.

The mirror was a small hand-held one, the handle black and engraved with flowers and vines, the oval glass tarnished with age. Dead insects lay around and on its reflective surface. It called to her in its simplicity, her skin prickling at its magick. Careful to avoid seeing her reflection, she wrapped the cloth fully around the mirror and lifted it out, relishing the charge that shot up her arm through her black gloves and made her fingers tingle.

"This is a surprise," came a soft voice over her shoulder.

She leapt away from the trunk, clutching her cloak to her as she spun.

The man who stood behind her wore a mask over the lower half of his face. A dark, hooded robe covered his hair and body. He held up gloved hands—one of them holding slender metal tools she recognized as lockpicks—as she stepped back from him.

"Apologies. I didn't expect to find the Magus of the Vale's vault such a popular destination tonight."

His voice was muffled by the mask, but still perfectly clear and polite. He slipped his lockpick tools under his robe and took a step back, as if to reassure her.

She wasn't fooled. Anyone skilled enough to break into the vault of the most powerful Magus on the continent—and who could sneak up on her despite her hearing—was dangerous indeed.

Oh, Gods. Not again. Not another retrieval gone wrong. Her heart pounded in her chest as she clutched the treasure she'd come for against her breast.

The man glanced around then back at her.

"You're alone?"

She stood silent and tense, the mirror a thrumming thing in her hands. She slipped it into one of her cloak's many pockets as he watched.

"That's good. I took care of the guards, but the Magus is in residence. We wouldn't want him to join us. They say three's a crowd."

"Who?" she asked before she could stop herself.

She watched his eyebrows arch. "Pardon?"

"Who says?"

He folded an arm across his waist and tapped the fore-finger of his other hand against his mask. "Good question. I doubt anyone has the answer. I certainly don't."

"Why do you care what they say then?"

A soft chuckle reached her. "I rarely do. Don't have the luxury, given my line of work."

"Which is stealing," she pointed out, her heart starting to slow as she realised he intended her no harm.

Thank the Gods. I couldn't do that again. To anyone.

"My Lady," he chided, "given our present activities, I find the unmistakable judgement in your tone at best inappropriate, and at worst, hypocritical."

A smile tried to break free, but she held it back.

You're wasting time you don't have dallying with this thief. Father will summon you back if you take much longer.

Summonings *hurt*. She avoided them at all costs. And if she angered him, what came after was even worse.

Now that she'd decided to leave father, it would not do to have him become suspicious. She had to bide her time until she found a way, and until then, he must believe nothing had changed and that she continued to be his obedient apprentice.

If she wasn't careful, this man would jeopardize that.

She thought of the Citadel, and the rainbow path glimmered into being, winding its way westward along the floor and through the vault's exterior wall.

The man drew in a sharp breath. "You have magick."

Iris stepped onto the path and watched the wall in front of her swirl open and part like windblown smoke.

"Leaving so soon? We haven't been properly introduced." He sounded amused and curious, as he stepped toward her.

Somewhere beneath her feet, she caught the sound of movement. Voices.

The man tensed, frowning.

He heard it too.

"I wouldn't linger if I were you."

He glanced at the path and then back at her. "Tell me your name."

"Good luck," she replied and strode to the wall. Just before she went through, she looked back and saw him trying to step on the path. He glanced up, giving her a rueful shake of his head, and she let a small smile crease her lips.

The path is mine, thief. You'll have to find your own way.

He faded from view, along with the room, and she was alone among familiar shifting white clouds, the faint whispers of the nebulous outside world closing in on her.

She chose to take her time and walk, head down as she thought about the thief and wondered whether he would escape the vengeance of the Magus of the Vale. The ghostly shadows of open fields, villages, people, and cities flitted past her—shifting through night and day as she crossed countries and continents unobserved.

When she eventually shook her thoughts free of the strange thief and lifted her gaze, she missed a step and came to a halt.

A grey outline of spindly limbs and two lumps she took for heads stood out against the white, nothing like the darker forms of people and the multicoloured haze of buildings. It hung from the side of a building in a busy city, a pewter mass no one else seemed to notice.

She stared at its mist-wrapped form, frowning.

The creature left the building in a swift bound and poked its limbs at the mist. It was much larger up close. At least several feet taller than her, and she was not a short woman.

With a sharp inhalation, Iris took a step back, almost off the path, which would have locked her into the place she stood, revealing her to all.

Revealing her to this creature.

How? How can it see me? Only the Aello and father knew of her gift, of her path.

Fear moved through her, spreading cold numbness. And Iris had no fear...

(*except for the Stone*)

...but whatever this thing was, she feared it down to her bones. Her reaction was irrational, impossible, and true as the taste of fruit and wine.

She watched the shape scuttle back and forth, as if looking for entry, and her heart pounded in her chest.

Get out of here before it finds a way.

She inched past the looming, many-limbed creature as it leaped at the path, then bounced off as if repelled. Relief unstopped her breath when she lost its shape in the white mists.

Long minutes later, a door solidified in front of her, and she pushed through, closing it behind her and leaning against it as if to keep out what she'd seen.

It didn't follow. It couldn't.

Was she sure of that?

She watched the path under her feet as it faded away.

Now I am.

A bulky shape rose from a dark corner of the room. "Iris?"

Eleni stepped forward into the circle of the light thrown by the one lamp Iris had lit before she left. The matriarch of the Aello frowned, the feathers atop her head standing up in alarm.

"What is it?"

Iris swallowed to ease her dry throat. "Nothing. I'm fine." She let go of the doorknob. "It's been a night of surprises."

Eleni's round yellow eyes took her in without blinking. "What happened? Did you not complete the Archmagus's retrieval?"

Of course. On to what matters most. Shoving the bitter thoughts down, Iris went to the lamps around the room and lit them one by one.

"I found what father wanted, yes." *And someone else as well.* It was on the tip of her tongue to tell Eleni about the thief, but at the last moment, she held back.

The thief was hers. Her secret. She'd never spoken to a human that wasn't father, and she didn't want to listen to Eleni's endless warnings about them. About the dangers of the outside world.

If she were going to leave and live as she saw fit, she would begin with this. Father and Eleni had no right to all she knew. All she did and thought. Not after the last retrieval.

Certainly not after the Stone.

Instead, she said, "I saw something strange on the way back."

"Oh?"

The room properly lit, Iris removed the mirror from her cloak, careful to lay it face down on her bed, still wrapped in its red velvet covering. She unclasped the dark woven cloak she used when breaking into guarded places and breathed a sigh as she stretched.

"Some sort of creature. It was off the path. I could not make it out. I think...I think it saw me."

Eleni's head bobbed. "Saw you? How could anything see you on the path?"

"I don't know." Iris sat on her bed with a frown. "It's never happened before."

Eleni cooed and ruffled her wings. "Are you...upset?"

Iris looked at her, surprised. Eleni rarely enquired after such tenuous things as feelings. She did her best when she sensed Iris was agitated—as might be the case if father was displeased—but it did not come naturally to her, or any other Aello. They preferred to tease and jibe and speak whatever came into their minds without hesitation.

Of course, Eleni had been trying harder since—

No. Don't think of that. Think of leaving.

"It was—unexpected. Eleni, what do you know of the Diviners?"

Eleni cocked her head, drawing closer, her long claws clicking on the stone floor. "Why do you ask this?"

"I thought it might be one of them. Father has not told me much about them."

"Because there is no need. They leave us alone, this far from the cities. We have nothing they want."

"They have powerful magick if they can see me and see my path." Iris plucked at her sheets, biting her lower lip. "Would they come after me?"

"Nonsense. They have no reason to seek you."

And yet, it was trying to find me. I'm sure of it.

"Diviners are human, in any case. This creature could not be one of them."

"What about their Gods?"

Eleni squawked in amusement. "Walking the open streets? Ridiculous!"

"But they're here, among us. The Diviners brought them through the Breach. Who knows what they look like?"

"Perhaps you should ask the Archmagus if this worries you so."

Familiar anger swept through her at the thought of asking father anything. But Eleni had a point. If anybody knew of the Diviners and their New Gods, it would be the Archmagus. He knew more of magick and the old and new denizens of this world than anyone, human or otherwise.

And he needed to know she had been seen.

A thought occurred to her. "Is that why you're here? Did he send you to wait for my return?"

Eleni stepped back, her wings lifting and falling. "You missed dinner."

Iris stared, uncomprehending.

Eleni nodded at the table near the doors to her balcony, where Iris liked to keep her books. In the dimness, a covered silver tray glinted. A pleasant shock went through her.

"Thank you," she said.

"You should see the Archmagus first. He's been waiting."

Iris sighed, crushing the sheet in her fist, her gaze on the tattoo of a chain twined around her wrist, peeking out from beneath her gloves.

"I hoped he'd be asleep."

"You know how long he's wanted the Enmity Mirror."

And like a good assistant, I bring it to him, just as he demands.

Iris tamped down the rage that rose in her as she stared at her wrist. She thought of the gold she'd hidden in her cloak, stolen from the collection of the Vale Magus before she took the Mirror. Destined to join the rest of the money she'd managed to ferret away in her mattress.

The thief was right. She was a hypocrite.

But not for much longer.

2

FORAGER

Father took the Mirror from her with gloved hands and laid it reverently on his desk. Light blazed everywhere in his study, even at this late hour. Tables and chairs and bookshelves and crates were crammed everywhere, piled high with books, potions, crystals, artefacts. The room was not as large as his Treasury below the Citadel, past the donjons. That cavern housed his main collection. His study held only those things he worked on at any point in time. And his books. Those that weren't too valuable or too dangerous to be left in the open.

He stroked the shape of the mirror's handle under the old velvet, his long grey hair falling forward to brush the desk.

"Did you have to kill anyone?"

His voice was deep, unconcerned, as if he enquired about the weather. She drew air against the sharp pain that went through her.

Never. Never again.

"I told you. I won't do that any longer."

"You've killed monsters and non-human guardians—"

"They were dangerous. A threat to my life. Or they had no mind of their own. They weren't *humans* doing a thankless job."

"Magickal relics are jealously guarded. How do you propose honouring this attack of conscience when you're assaulted or challenged in the future?"

By not stealing for you any longer.

"I'll find a way."

He looked up at her, eyebrows raised above dark eyes in a face tanned as old leather. "Will you change your skin, Iris? Change who you are? What you've already done?"

"You know I have never deliberately hurt anyone!"

"No animal does. But lions must eat, and prey is there to be eaten."

"I'm not an animal," she ground out between her teeth. "I'm not Aello, and I'm not heartless." *Like you.*

He sighed, as if exhausted. "If this is about last year, I did what I thought—"

"I think someone saw me on the path," she blurted, desperate not to hear him. She couldn't bear it. He could not know the depth of her anger and resolve, and she might reach out and throttle him if she had to listen to his lies yet again. Taste the bitterness of it on her tongue.

He stilled his stroking of the mirror, his gaze unblinking as an Aello's. "You think?"

She described what had happened. He listened without a word or movement.

"Could it be a Diviner, or one of their Gods?"

He leaned against the wooden back of his chair, his fingers drumming against the desk. "It was one of the Diviner's pets. They sniff out magick and...other things. I thought the last of them died during the war."

"But one is alive?"

He met her gaze, his thoughtful and unreadable. "Iris, you must be cautious from now on. You must do whatever is necessary to protect yourself. If the Foragers are still around, they are a danger to you. To anyone with your magick."

It was a strange night indeed. First, two encounters. Then, both Eleni and the Archmagus expressing concern for her.

Too little, too late.

"I won't kill again, father."

He tried to cover his wince at her use of the title, but she saw it anyway. She glanced at the door across the room, a shudder going through her.

"No matter what you do to me. I mean it."

"So dramatic. I'm only concerned for your safety, Iris."

"Then use your Rebound incantation and summon me back. Or stop sending me after these relics."

"I cannot." He waved a hand. "In time, you'll understand I do all this to keep us safe."

She scoffed. "You grow your power for your own hubris."

"If that were all," he said in a soft voice. "You would know."

He was right, curse him. And the taste of it overwhelmed her senses.

As she watched, he lifted the mirror, closed his eyes, and whispered. Then he peeled the cloth away and looked into it without speaking for nearly a minute.

The Enmity Mirror showed you your greatest threat, she knew. But to look into it was to bring that threat into being. There would be no escaping the confrontation. She didn't know why the Archmagus wanted the mirror so. He only ever told her enough about her retrievals and the relics she handled to know how not to hurt herself. But he'd warned her not to look into it, and she'd taken his warnings seriously, as she always did.

"What do you see?" she asked, curious.

He put the mirror face down and took a breath. When he met her gaze again, he was calm as though nothing had occurred.

"You must rest now. Find Eleni and send her to me."

She walked away without a word, careful not to let him see her frustration at his predictable avoidance of her question.

In the morning, he was gone, and Eleni could only shrug and tell her, "He has gone to Vale. He returns in a week. Till then, you are to remain in your quarters."

A prisoner. As always. She stared at her tattoos and clenched her fist, watching her flesh shift beneath them, her thoughts filled with three things. The creature, the Archmagus...and the polite thief she'd left behind.

Four nights passed with no word. Not unusual for father. He was often away without explanation, only to return with new artefacts, or new information as to where to find more.

The first night, Iris went down to the study while the Aello slumbered, hoping to find it unlocked. But as she suspected, he'd not placed his new artefact in the Treasury below the Citadel yet. The door was locked. Frustrated, she stayed as long as she dared, muttering incantations and trying the handle, but it remained solidly shut, preventing her from carrying out the same search she attempted every time the Archmagus left the Citadel. Somewhere in her father's study was the key that would allow her to leave the Citadel. Since the previous year, she'd searched the Treasury many times and found nothing. She was sure what she needed was hidden in the study. But the Archmagus had never left it unsecured, and this time was no exception.

With no way to free herself, she went back to outwardly doing as she preferred, while inwardly biding her time. She tended her garden, visited the hatchling's rookery to play with the new chicks and read her novels.

She was laying on her bed, reading a collection of her favourite poems, when a heavy feeling came over her. It smothered her with intense suddenness, making her breaths harsh and her chest tight. The book fell from her hands to the crumpled sheets as she doubled over, blinking against sudden tears in her eyes. Despair climbed into her throat like a live thing.

She tumbled off the bed and got to her feet, no real thoughts in her mind except to get out, to get away. She flung open the doors to the rose garden and stood gasping, trying to draw air into her lungs.

What's happening to me? What is this?

She wondered if this was what being ill felt like. She'd never experienced it, but the Aello sometimes did, and when that happened, Eleni and a few of the other mothers would separate the sick from the flock and tend them.

Eleni. She had been with father the longest. She had seen much and might know what this was.

Iris turned on weak legs and went to the door, wrenching it open even as her stomach roiled.

A huge shape barrelled through, and she stumbled back from it, crashing into her table of books and tumbling some to the floor.

Elbows braced against the rocking table, she tried to breathe through a suddenly constricting throat. Alarmed squawks came from deeper in the building as the intruder leapt on her bed, hissing loudly.

It was taller than her by far, a mottled brown, white and grey, and lightly furred. Spindly legs ended in delicate paws that must have been quieter than a cat's to hide its approach from her. At least a dozen limbs sprang from the creature's triple-segmented thorax, and two heads twisted on short stalks, as if searching for something.

Each head was a blind, furred oval with two large vertical slits and one gaping, rose-petal pink mouth that sucked at the air with a gentle hissing noise. The slits trembled, expanded, and both heads snapped around in her direction. The pink tunnel of its mouth changed to blood-red, and the moist flesh rippled continuously. It stood up on six limbs, heads almost brushing the high ceiling as it thrust its belly up and forward, and instinct sent her to the floor.

Something thudded into the wall behind her as she rolled toward the door before getting to her knees.

An outraged caw came from the doorway and she turned to see Leo, one of the armed Aello guards, black feathers an angry, erect halo circling his face.

"Stay back," she shouted.

It was too late. Leo had already fluttered into the room, slashing forward with his sword.

The creature leapt for the stone ceiling, ran two steps across it, and crashed down onto the guard, hugging him to it, its stomach tight against his back. The sword in his hand crashed to the floor.

Leo screeched. Despite the waves of nausea and pain that made her gasp and tremble, Iris heard the Aello answer his cry with the rhythm of many wings on the air. The creature—she knew now it must be the same one that had seen her on the rainbow path—stood over his twitching body, faces toward her, the red insides of its hissing mouths rippling faster.

How did it find me?

She stood, keeping her movement slow, one hand over the fiery ache of her stomach.

It scuttled around to face her, towering over her again. She saw clear, slick fluid on its stomach as a gap opened and closed rhythmically, birthing a black, pointed tip. And under it, the blunt, rough end of another barb rose out of Leo's back.

Her entire body leaned toward the thing, as if pulled toward the creature. Battling the rising urge to go to it, she began to understand that *this* was the source of her sudden illness. Caught in a vice controlled by this being, malevolence and hunger buffeted her. Fear pebbled her skin. Waves of increasing pain swept over her, sapping her strength inexorably into the open, hissing mouths.

It's weakening me before it attacks me. Feeds on me.

She put her hand against the wall for support. Alone in her room, she had not put her gloves on and the cold stone leached warmth from her. Reminded her of her greatest weapon. The one she'd vowed not to use again.

The creature's limbs twitched, four nose-slits wide, heads bent over her, hissing, hissing.

"Don't make me do this," she whispered.

I don't want to die before I've lived.

Claws clattered against the stone floor outside. The Aello's voices rose in angry caws and squawks. The heads turned to the open doorway as a figure appeared in it. Iris took a deep, painful breath as the Archmagus met her gaze with his dark one. And she knew. *She knew.*

"Father," she said hoarsely. "*Please.*"

The creature leapt at her with feline suddenness. She held her arms out, fingers spread wide, and braced herself as legs strong and thin as rope closed around her, blocking the Archmagus from view.

Her hands sank into fur softer than the down on a chick's body, clutched for a mere second against the heaving thorax. The scent of burned grass choked her. She held it away from her, elbows wide to keep its legs from closing around her and dragging her to the ground.

The creature shuddered, the hissing louder above her head. Panicked. Closing her eyes as long legs jerked and jolted around her, she tightened her grip until she felt the rippling under its fur, the rapid, pained contractions of muscles. She heard the patter of liquid hitting the floor, faster and faster.

She held it aloft, its body growing lighter with every moment that passed. For the first time, her own suffering began to ease, breath leaving her body in a rush, then returning with the burned smell layered on it like smoke.

She shoved the thing away from her and stumbled into the garden, where she retched into the sweet, thorny roses until there was nothing left in her stomach.

Until Eleni came to her and carefully dropped her cloak over her shoulders and her gloves at her feet. Her mouth bitter and trembling, she put her gloves on and pulled her cloak close.

"Leo?" she asked, her voice hoarse.

"Dead," Eleni said in her blunt way. "Poison."

Iris nodded, her heart squeezing in her chest. She'd known Leo as a hatchling. He was impulsive, boastful and a prankster. He was also fierce, protective, and brave. He'd given his life for her, the first among them to die in a long time. She stood back from the roses and blinked back the moisture in her eyes. The Aello would not abide tears for someone who died a warrior.

"I'm sorry, Eleni."

"He did his job. He protected us." Eleni stepped back as Iris turned to face her. "So did you," she added.

Anger rushed up from somewhere deep inside her—lava escaping a vent. She forced herself to look through the doors into her room.

Leo and the creature had already been taken away. His sword lay next to a huge puddle of black ichor lumpy with bits of flesh and furred skin. The dead creature would have been a shrivelled version of itself, blood reduced to ichor, muscles petrified, curled and twisted like dried branches. And the pain it would have endured...

It would have killed you. You had no choice.

There was always a choice. And the Archmagus had made sure to force this one.

"I did what *he* should have," she said out loud. She narrowed her eyes at Eleni. "Surely you understand that?"

Eleni let her wings lift and fall. "He would never let us come to harm."

"He let Leo come to harm."

"Leo knew what was expected of him."

"He stood there, Eleni. And did *nothing*."

"He didn't need to." Eleni tilted her head, examining her with unblinking eyes. "You are who you are."

Shuddering at the truth in those words, Iris went back into the room, skirting the puddle and its death-stink, her cloak clutched to her throat.

Father was already at his desk when she found him in his study. She slammed the door behind her and stalked up to him, rage spilling out into her blood, fired in the kiln of her heart.

"Why?" she bit out. "Why, father?"

A tiny frown wrinkled his forehead. "You know the answer to that."

"You know I never wanted to kill again. I begged for your help." Her breath caught, hot and thick with tears she could not shed. "You stood there and let it attack me."

"I let you see how childish you've been. How ridiculous. You are not some gentle maiden, Iris. You are my apprentice. When you wield magick—life and death—you must be sure of yourself in both. You felt yourself in danger and you protected yourself. There is nothing wrong in this."

She scoured his face with her gaze as a terrible certainty rose within her. "You brought it here. To teach me a lesson."

"I had to deal with it, Iris. It had caught wind of you. Foragers do not forget. You're lucky it was a young one, not yet attached to a Diviner."

"You deliberately brought something that dangerous into the Citadel and now Leo is dead because of it!"

The Archmagus slammed his fist down on his desk. She took a step back, surprised at his rare display of temper.

"Every Aello understands they must protect the Citadel against intruders. Leo gave his life for that. You took a life for the same reason. In this world, we are all we have, the only ones we can trust. It is past time you accepted that, as the rest of us have."

"You expect me to believe an Archmagus wouldn't have been able to destroy that thing where you found it, instead of bringing it here?"

He rose to his feet, his lips curled. "I would never risk the Citadel if there was another way."

"But you admit when you left here, you intended to return with it? And now Leo is dead because of that decision?"

"We were in danger. I went to deal with the threat. Leo's death only proves I was right to go."

"You mean *you* were in danger." She clenched her fists at her side. "It's always about you."

He narrowed his eyes at her. "What affects me affects us all."

She paused as something else occurred to her. "Was this about what you saw in the Mirror?"

The slightest twitch of his eye let her know she was on the right track.

"You saw something? Someone?"

The Archmagus was silent for a long moment before slowly sinking into his chair. She waited, braced for the usual dismissal.

"I didn't find him," he said. "And that is not good news."

She raised her eyebrows, shocked at a rare moment of honesty from him. "Who is he? Did the Mirror tell you?"

"It shows you where your enemy is at that moment. Nothing more. By the time I arrived in the Vale, he had moved on."

"So, you do know who he is?"

He hesitated before nodding. "A Merchant Lord. Headed home to his people after a successful trading trip."

"Did you know him before? Have you an idea why he would be your enemy."

The Archmagus shook his head, his gaze seeing something past her shoulder. "I have never seen him before, nor heard his name. I have had no dealings with his people. But the Mirror is never wrong. I must find him before he finds me."

She frowned, her mind racing. "You're leaving again?"

"I must. We are not safe until I find this man."

"Will you kill him when you find him?"

His gaze met hers immediately. "That is no concern of yours."

She had had enough. She leaned forward, making sure he was focused on her. "Hear me now, father. You have manipulated me for the last time. I will not be party to a man's murder. Do not come to me for that."

"Understand me, Iris," he replied softly. "You will do as you are told if you wish to remain safe in this Citadel. Or you can try to face on your own things that make the Forager seem but a pleasant dream."

Iris tasted the sweetness of his words before the bitterness of her decision consumed it.

"We will not speak of this again," he added.

She straightened, her resolve iron-firm. "No, we will not."

As expected, Eleni and the Aello were gathered in the main rookery, just outside the entrance to the donjon and the Treasury.

They fluttered away from her as she entered, their harsh cries filling the air. Leo lay on the floor in the centre of the enormous, vaulted room, wings folded over his chest.

Eleni stood over him, stroking his feathers into place. She didn't look up as Iris entered, only said, "Finished with your fight?"

"Don't start," Iris said, her throat tight. "I'm here for Leo."

"*He* doesn't know that," one of them called down.

"Dead is dead," another agreed.

"What was the fight about?" asked a third.

"What's it always about, these days?" Eleni answered.

The flock was all fluttering wings and chirps for a few moments.

"Glad you killed it, girl." She looked up to see Belen, Eleni's long-time mate, edging closer along one of the many thick wooden beams studding the walls and ceiling. His grey and white feathers stirred in the wind from the small air holes in the outer wall. "Does he know what it was? How it found us?"

"He called it a Forager. He brought it here," Iris said, not bothering to hide her anger. "He intended for me to kill it."

"Did a fine job of it too," laughed one of the guards. The flock laughed with him. "Poor Leo. Not so much, him. Dropped his sword and that was that."

"No, it wasn't," Iris said, her voice loud. She spun in a circle, meeting their gazes. "He came in there determined to protect me. That thing was more than twice his size and he never blinked. He was brave and he's gone, and I will *never* understand why you all can't just weep when one of us dies, *just once.*"

Her voice echoed in the shocked silence that filled the room. The faint cries of the fledgelings below, near the Treasury, reproached the words she hadn't known she was going to say.

"You know that's not how we are," Eleni said in the quiet. "We're not weak as humans."

Like you, Iris heard, without her saying it.

"When it's your time, it's your time," a guard added, scratching his wing with a spear.

"Better to go out fighting," another agreed.

"Will you always defend him? Even when he gets one of us killed?" Iris asked Eleni. "Can none of you see how wrong this is?"

"Death comes to everyone, girl. No death is better than one that protects the flock. By the North Wind, she's always been a strange one," croaked one of the elders, shifting heavily on her perch.

"Foundlings," a mother agreed, ducking her head several times. "It's always hard when you don't know what kind of nest they came from."

Her words might as well have been an arrow. Iris drew in a painful breath as Eleni silenced the mother with a screech.

"You know better, by now," she addressed the flock with the full power of her authority. They settled into immediate silence. "She saved your feathers, and this is how you talk?"

"Didn't mean anything by it," the mother said, wings closed around herself. "We all know she's not one of us. But she's done right by us all, and the Archmagus loves her like a daughter."

The flock cooed in agreement.

"Apologies, Iris," a few of them chorused. She closed her eyes and breathed deep, searching for patience and grace, and finding she had none left.

None left to deal with their constant barbs. The ways they teased endlessly about how different she was. She was tired of trying to fit in. To not be the foundling they found curious and exasperating at best, disloyal at worst.

She opened her eyes to meet Eleni's direct gaze. "Iris," the only mother she'd ever known cautioned, "you know our ways. It's not a time for tears."

"Not nearly! He was a great one for pranks. Remember the time he..." One of the Ciceros started in on the memory-sharing as the flock listened, contributing little comments and questions as he went. Preserving the memory of Leo in this moment.

Because after this moment passed, they would not speak of him again. The flock had no time for the dead. The living took up all their focus.

She had no choice but to remember. He would forever be the nestmate she'd lost because father wanted to teach her a lesson. Well, she was done with him—with the Archmagus. Because that was who he was in those moments. She was done with his lessons, and with anyone who thought the best thing she could do in life was submit to whatever father thought best.

She'd tried so hard for so long. But in the end, it was a relief to let it all go.

She turned away.

"Where are you going? The Archmagus has to give his blessing before we Burn."

"You don't need me for that, Eleni," Iris said without turning around. "You don't need me at all."

She went back to her room with her head held high, ignoring the little jabs they threw after her.

"She's mad."

"Nothing new there."

"Needs thicker skin that one." Uproarious laughter greeted that joke; the sound and sentiment burned her ears and hardened her determination.

Once the Archmagus left to hunt his enemy, she would try again to search his study until she found the key to her chains, then leave to make her own way. The Forager had taught her that danger could find her anywhere. She might as well meet it on her own terms.

3

MAGNIFICENT CREATURE

Three days later, father was finally gone, and Iris could breathe again.

She was taking the evening air on her private balcony, waiting for it to be late enough to put her plans in motion, when the thief dropped down from the wall that towered above her, landing silently on a dirt path bordered by rose bushes. She watched as he unhooked the sleeve of his shirt from some thorns, only to freeze when he saw her sitting on her bench, book still open in her lap.

He wore no hood this time, but she knew his body immediately. She took in his dark eyes and hair, and lips that curved as though holding back laughter at some secret joke. The belt that hung low on his waist carried a small pouch and various tools. He raised his eyebrows at her.

"Well," he said in a voice as kind as his eyes, "I didn't expect to see you here."

"Obviously," Iris replied, her hand shaking a little as she closed her book. His voice was warm, as though they were friends long separated and it gave him joy to see her. She'd never been greeted like that before. Father abhorred public gestures and words of affection.

"This isn't what it appears," he said as she stood. Light sparkled around her like a mirror struck by sunlight, more than enough to read by at that hour.

"It appears you've somehow climbed the walls of Citadel and entered my garden, with the intention of stealing whatever treasure you can carry."

"Truthfully," he said, teeth flashing in a smile as dazzling as her light, "I'm only interested in one bit of treasure. Given the wealth contained within these walls, surely you could spare a tiny donation to the cause of keeping me from the poorhouse?"

Bitterness slicked the back of her throat as she let her gaze travel from the top of his neatly trimmed hair, down his fine-spun black shirt and breeches, to his sturdy boots. He was taller than her, and though his hands were gloved as hers, she could see the strength in his bared forearms. She held her book to her chest, her lips a compressed line, as much to convey her disbelief as to prevent herself from answering his smile with her own. "Forgive me if I have trouble believing you've done more than walk past the poorhouse in your time."

He took a step forward, his chuckle so soft she almost missed it. "Would you believe I was born in one?"

"Men such as yourself often have unsavoury origins." Her voice was calm, reflecting none of the awareness that made her skin goosebump in his presence.

He took another step forward, his eyes wide with surprise. "Men such as myself? And what would you know of men like me?"

She steeled herself not to move, not to rise to his words. She was no fool and he was a liar. There was only one reason for an intruder to enter the Citadel at this hour.

Still, something in him called to her. She couldn't deny she liked him.

You know nothing about him, and you stand here trading words instead of raising the alarm.

Father no longer deserved her loyalty though, and she would not help the Aello hurt this man.

"You should leave," she said, "If you do, I won't tell anyone you were here. You can go with your life and no-one the wiser."

He was almost in front of her. She would be a dark shape to him, draped in light, and she drew back into the shadows to stay hidden a little longer. She cast a quick glance at the open doors that led into her bedroom, and the warm glow of the lamps that emanated from it. He followed her gaze then met hers again.

"You weren't supposed to be here," he said again. "Don't you all go below once the sun sets?"

Not me. Never me.

"You won't succeed," she said instead. "The Aello will know you're coming."

"That," he said, "is what I'm counting on."

She gasped, sweetness replacing bitterness on her tongue, making her scared for him. Perhaps he was ill, or suicidal. He didn't seem the type, but she'd only just met him, how would she know otherwise?

"You won't get ten feet once you leave my room."

"Maybe."

"They'll tear you to pieces."

"We'll see." He'd backed her into the shadows near the perimeter without her realising it and she came to an abrupt halt.

Stop. This is stupid. He's not the dangerous one here.

"Why are you warning me away instead of attacking me?" he breathed, and she smelled him for the first time, sweet as figs, tart with sweat.

She clutched her book harder, his words piercing her like pins. "I'm not one of them."

"Clearly." His gaze dropped. "What are you reading?"

He was so close she could smell the slightest trace of spirits on his breath. "What?"

He raised a finger and tapped at her book. She jumped away from him. "Don't!"

He frowned. "I didn't—"

"You can't touch me," she said in a rush, "Don't touch me. I'll kill you, and it will be horrible."

She took a trembling breath as he stepped back for the first time.

"You want to kill me?" he asked, his voice serious. Considering.

"No!" She shook her head, frantic. "But you'll die if you touch me."

He smiled then, a cheeky flash as he reverted to charm. "There are worse deaths than the embrace of a beautiful woman."

A flush spread over her body even as her heart dropped. He was playing with her, the way the Aello sometimes did. She'd thought him different.

Why did I think that? I don't know him.

"You can't possibly see what I look like," she pointed out. "You're just trying to keep me from raising the alarm, but flattery isn't necessary. I've already said you can go."

His laugh was gentle. "I've seen you quite clearly since I landed on this side of the wall, I assure you. A mage spelled my eyes years ago. I see like an owl in the dark, and an eagle in the day."

His words froze her in place, and she didn't resist as he took the book from her and read the spine. "The Bard Left Bare. Poetry. A favourite of yours?"

"Yes." Her voice was so hoarse she barely recognized it.

"Mine as well." His gaze met hers and she saw something in their depths she didn't want to believe.

He likes you too.

"What's your name?"

"Iris. What's yours?"

"Iris." He tasted her name as though it were fine spirits. "I'll be going now. Stay here. No-one should know you saw me. I wouldn't like you to get in trouble."

She understood then there would be no dissuading him. Her heart wanted to hold him there with her, alive, warm and charming, but he was determined to go and nothing she said would stop him.

They'll take him and that will be the end of the only person who's ever really seen me.

The words left her before she realised she was going to speak. "I won't forget you."

He paused and she saw the corner of a smile. "I hope not. I pride myself on being quite memorable."

He slipped inside and she stood on the balcony, clutching her book and hoping against hope.

Only to have that hope dashed a long while later when a faint, angry cry came to her ears, telling her he had failed, and the Aello had him.

She dropped the book, her mind made up.

Not him. I've known enough death.

She flew out of her room and down the hall, following the thin screeches and thrills that rose up from the donjon. Rushing past the Aello pouring into the rookery, she reached the Treasury and stopped inside the doors, a few feet away from a teeming melee illuminated by flickering torchlight.

"Leave him!" she shouted.

One of the Aello broke off from the fight and cawed at her, brown-black wings spread high, talons distended. "Go, Iris. We have him already."

She saw the man struggling on the floor as talons slashed down at him, snagging cloth and clicking against the wooden floor when they missed. Blood flowed from a gash in his bared shoulder. She caught a glimpse of his eyes between the crush of feathers before the Aello closed in again, screeching and cawing in anger.

With a cry of warning, she flung her arms up and shifted her shoulders. She'd left her transparent cloak in her room and the blinding brilliance of her wings as they unfurled around her made the Aello gasp and shield their eyes. She used that moment to charge them.

The Aello scattered as the doorway filled with their male brethren, their weapons at the ready, chest feathers ruffled. Angry and alarmed, the flock hovered well above her or returned to their roosts, gripping with strong bared legs that ended in curved claws.

The air filled with caws and screeches as Iris hung above the man, careful not to touch him as her wings beat the air, making a protective cage around him. His torn shirt fluttered in the wind she stirred. Her light illuminated the scratches and wounds on his face and chest, and made his blood bright red. He held feathers, dragged from his attackers during the fight, tight in both hands. Yet he smiled at her as though nothing out of the ordinary had happened.

As though she hadn't just defied the only family she'd ever known to save his life.

"Iris!" Eleni screeched at her. "What madness is this?"

She looked up at the matriarch of the Aello, desperation making her almost breathless. "I can't let you hurt him."

"He's a thief!"

"I object," the man said in an amused voice. "I haven't stolen a thing. I never even made it to the door of the Treasury."

"Quiet," Iris hissed at him. "You'll make it worse."

"Why are you doing this?" they both asked her at once, Eleni in anger, the man with curiosity in his tone.

She shook her head, unable to answer when she had no idea herself. "Give him to me, Eleni. I'll make sure he doesn't come back."

"He must die! You know that. There are rules. *His* rules."

"He's not here," Iris pleaded, not looking away from the dark pools of the man's eyes. There was something in them that made her throat tight and her voice shake. "He doesn't have to know."

A raucous chorus greeted this, and one of the Aello spoke in a disgusted tone. "Stupid gosling. He *always* knows."

"You heard him," she looked around at everyone, "he didn't take anything. You don't have to kill him for climbing a wall."

"Even if we didn't need to know how he got in, we would have to make an example of him," Eleni shot back. "Stop this, Iris."

"You're a magnificent creature," the man breathed at her and she dropped her gaze again. There was a dreaminess to his look now, as though his mind was taken up by deeply pleasurable thoughts.

More likely it's the toxins. He's very strong to still be conscious when so many Aello claws have pierced him.

"How are you even here?"

"Why do you keep asking me questions when I'm trying to save your life?"

"Because you're fascinating," he said, shifting his head as if making himself more comfortable. "I've never met your like. Few did before. Few ever will now."

The knowledge in his voice arrested her and she released a shaky breath. "What do you mean?"

"Iris." The voice came from the direction of the doorway and she glanced up to see swords and spears pointed at her. "Move away, or we will make you." The yellow and black depths of Belen's eyes were flat and without pity.

"You don't know who you are," he said beneath her, a thread of shock in his voice.

She glanced back at him, frowning. "Of course, I do. I'm Iris."

She saw his expression shift and his body tense.

"Damn it." His gaze met hers, frustration and a strange determination in them. "Not now."

"What?"

He bit his lip. "Iris—"

She blinked and he was gone, leaving her hovering over a dark puddle and a lone Aello feather.

Eleni had her locked in her room, but not before she lectured Iris on what would be done. What had to be done.

"You know how he prizes loyalty," she said, her voice and eyes hard, her talons clicking as she opened and closed her hands. "What you have done—it's inexcusable. Treachery."

Iris sat on her small bed, numb. She stared at her gloved hands as they held her cloak in her lap.

Why, why, why did I do that? He never even told me his name.

A few charming words, a beautiful smile, was all it took. It would be a long time before the Archmagus trusted her again. Before she would have another chance at escape.

And yet, she could find no regret within herself. No remorse.

Only that he didn't know what it meant when he spoke to me. That he didn't feel what I did.

How the world had burned bright and still for those moments he looked at her on the balcony, among the roses.

With a groan, she dropped the cloak and covered her face with her hands. Eleni chittered, satisfied that she was appropriately chastised.

"Humans are tricky. Now you understand why the Archmagus chose to keep you here, safe and hidden. Our kind do not belong out there."

Iris lowered her hands, an old anger blazing through her. "And yet, the moment he wants something, who does he send into the world to get it?"

"Unfair!" Eleni replied, the feathers at the crown of her head standing up in annoyance. "He needs those items to grow his power, so he can protect the Citadel. Protect you. He could have let you die when he found you all those years ago. He took you in and look how you repay him. So ungrateful!"

"How am I ungrateful?" she cried, anger making her eyes burn. "I do whatever he asks. He shows me a drawing and I retrieve the item, no matter how far away, no matter the danger. And my reward is to be trapped here as though I have no heart, no mind of my own. And when I...could not hurt others as he told me to? He hurt *me* instead. *You* hurt me too, Eleni."

"For your own safety! And now you've proven you can't be trusted." Eleni's wings flapped as she paced. "Stubborn, strange creature! The Archmagus has feared you would be false for some time. He will believe he has no choice now."

Fear shuddered through her. "What do you mean?"

Eleni's flat shiny gaze swept over her. "You can guess. You know how harsh he can be. He returns within the week. That will be your reckoning."

Iris stared. "You would let him do it? Again?"

Eleni bobbed her head, opened and closed her mouth, then turned and marched from the room.

Tears burned behind Iris's eyes, but as usual, she could not let them fall. Instead, she lay down and stared at the stone walls, her mind empty.

She didn't know when her eyes closed. She only knew when she opened them again, her lamps had burned off all their oil, the sun was high in the sky and the largest man she'd ever seen was crouched by the side of her bed.

She scrambled back, her vision tilting and her mind dizzy with the sudden movement. He shook his shaggy head at her, and the look in his eyes—a look that pleaded with her not to cry out—made her hesitate. He took a breath, his gaze roving over her.

"He's right, blast him," the man rumbled in a soft voice like far-off thunder. "Skin like dark velvet. Wings like moonlight."

Her heart missed a beat at the gentleness in his tone.

There is a strange, hairy, bull of a man in your room—the second to enter the Citadel in a day—and that is what you focus on? Your brains are addled, Iris.

"Who...?" she said on a choked breath.

The man rose to his full impressive height, looming over her bed.

"You are Iris," he said rather than asked.

"How do you know my name?" she demanded, closing her wings around herself defensively.

"Meri told me." He watched as she frowned. He wore brown robes with sleeves to his wrists, and his hair grew long and thick to his shoulders. His face was angles and hard lines, a jutting shelf of a jaw shadowed by a beard, and eyebrows thick as caterpillars over sky-blue eyes.

"Meri?"

He grunted and put his hands on his hips. She stared, distracted by the breath of shoulders and chest that pressed against the fabric of his clothes.

"He never introduced himself?"

The amused benevolence in his eyes was completely at odds with his fearsome appearance. Then she focused on his words. "He? Do you mean..."

His chest rose and fell in a soft sigh. "Flippant to the point of rudeness? Came over the wall, made one hell of a mess and vanished without a trace?"

A smile tugged at the corners of her lips.

"I shall not indulge in his worst habits then." The man bowed gracefully, and she saw the points of two horns twisting out of his glossy dark hair. "I am Achelous of Ingmar. You've already met my...companion, Meri, and for that I humbly apologize."

A short huff of laughter escaped her as he straightened with a knowing look in his eyes, an answering smile curving his mouth. She caught her breath at the way it transformed his features into rough beauty, her chest tight.

He heard her gasp and misread it. "No, don't be afraid." He spread his large hands to show he meant no harm and she slid off the other side of the bed and stood.

Understanding lit his eyes. "You've nothing to fear." She watched as he bent and swept a hand at the bed. His hand went through it, only to reappear when he withdrew it.

"You see, I'm not really here. I can't hurt you and you can't hurt me."

Meri had told him then. She edged around the bed and went to him, her heart pulsing with excitement in her throat and at her wrists.

"How are you doing this?"

"Parlour trick really," he said in his rumbling voice, pleased at her interest. "I can cast myself to any place Meri or I have visited before."

"You're...connected?" she said standing in front of him. Despite her height, the top of her head came to just below his shoulders.

Achelous sighed. "He's been in my charge for years now."

"What does that mean?"

His smile was gentle. "It's too long a story for the moment."

"Are you both mages, to be able to do such things?"

He laughed under his breath. "Mages, no. We have magick, yes."

She frowned, her mind crowding with questions. "Why are you here?"

"To apologize." His deep voice vibrated pleasurably, just under her skin. "Meri didn't intend to embroil you in his ill-considered venture. Once I saw to his wounds and he'd come back to himself, he wished me to make sure you were not harmed and that you knew he regretted whatever trouble he might have brought you."

"Is he gravely injured? Is that why he didn't come himself?" She shouldn't care, she knew, but she could not bear the thought of him being hurt.

"He'll make a full recovery soon. Although after this latest nonsense, a little suffering on his part would be a good thing."

"Why did he come here? Doesn't he know how dangerous the Citadel is?"

Achelous folded his hands inside his long sleeves, exasperation tightening his features. "You've met him twice now. Does he seem the type to run from danger?"

"But I don't understand what he hoped to gain. Why did he risk his life to break in here? And how did he escape?"

"Because he's impulsive and has a death wish," he replied, with a twist of his lips and a roll of his eyes. "He accepted a ridiculous dare from a mage to retrieve Aello feathers. As for his escape—a Rebound incantation. He cast it beforehand. It takes you back to the place of its invocation after a set amount of time has passed."

The same spell the Archmagus had used to summon her for years. Whenever she left the Citadel on one of his missions, it was how he made sure she returned when he wished. Meri was gifted and clever to know such a rare incantation. But then she'd already guessed that.

"Are you?" Achelous asked.

"Am I what?"

"Unharmed."

She sank onto the bed, the excitement leaching from her body as she remembered what Eleni had said. Achelous made a sound in his throat.

"By the Gods. He's gotten you into trouble, hasn't he?"

She shrugged. "I chose to try to protect him. It's not his fault. He told me to stay out of it."

"It's entirely his fault." His voice was still quiet, but there was real disgust there. And concern. Concern for...her? Her gaze flew to his face.

"Why does it matter to either of you what happens to me?"

Achelous frowned so that his brows almost met. He looked uncertain how to answer and the longer he stayed silent, the surer she became she'd read too much into his words.

He cursed, his voice soft and vicious. "Meri's never asked me to do anything like this before. With him it's usually in and out, and on his way. But now I've met you..."

Her heart pounded so hard she thought he could hear it. "Yes?"

He looked away, fidgeting with his sleeves. "I think perhaps I know why he worried. You don't belong here, do you?"

She hesitated, not sure how to answer. "I've been here all my life."

"You don't *belong* here," he repeated, his voice careful, and this time she was the one who looked away.

No. I don't belong. I never have.

That was why she had planned to leave. But now she'd betrayed the Archmagus, there was no telling when that would be.

"It's the only home I've ever had," she said.

"You mean it's the only place you know."

"No," she said. "I've...been to other lands. I've stood on the walls. On a clear day, I can see the town. I know there's more out there."

"And you wish to see it?"

She should deny it, but she didn't want to. Father would return soon, and she might never see Meri or Achelous again. She didn't want lies between them. Lies tasted bitter in her mouth and she hated them as much as she hated her captivity.

"All my life I've wished to see it," she admitted.

"You could leave. Fly from here. Why haven't you?"

She hesitated, searching his face. But there was nothing but curiosity and compassion there, and so she pushed back the long sleeves of her dress and showed him her wrists and the chains tattooed around them. His eyes narrowed and a snort escaped him, an angry sound.

"You're imprisoned here?"

"Fath—the Archmagus does not wish me to wander. He says the outside world is no place for me."

Achelous began to pace, his face grim. "He's trapped you in a Citadel known far and wide for the dangerous creatures, spells and potions he's collected. How is this place better?"

"You misunderstand. He's not only worried about what will happen to me." She swallowed and lifted her eyes to meet his. "He's worried about what will happen to others. My touch is death. I wear gloves and my cloak, but accidents have happened. I have no desire to hurt anyone, but if people knew what I was, they might attack me. Kill me."

He stopped pacing and she saw from the clench of his jaw that father was right. For years she'd harboured a fantasy of freedom. Of flying away to see the vast lands she'd only visited for a few short minutes. Experience the emotions her beloved poetry spoke of. But the flicker of understanding Achelous had not been able to hide tightened her chest.

"He's right, isn't he? People will try to kill me. Because I'm not one of them."

"Not all of them," Achelous said. Sighing he turned to face her, one hand tugging through his hair. "But yes. Some people fear what is different. Fear the unknown. Some people take what they want because they can. Kill because they can. But that isn't all there is. The world is bigger than the bad things in it."

"But don't you see?" She pulled a glove off, exposing the diamond-hard tips of pearlescent claws at the end of her fingers. "I'm one of the bad things."

Anger flashed over his face. He opened his mouth to say something and she heard the click of claws on the floor in the hall. She stared at the door.

"Someone's coming."

But when she turned back to Achelous, she discovered herself alone.

4

A Bond Between Us

The next night, Eleni sent someone else with her dinner and Iris felt her rejection like a slap across her face. Of course, she would not come. She would not argue over what was certain. No Aello would. And it was certain that once the Archmagus returned, Eleni would be expected to assist him in Iris' punishment.

She stared at the food with her hands fisted so tightly in her lap, her claws tore at her skin. The tiny crescents of pain grounded her, kept the scream in her throat from rising into the air. In the end, she left the plate untouched and threw her balcony doors open, striding into the sweet evening wind...

...and came to an abrupt halt as the tall shape sitting on the edge of the high wall around her balcony turned to face her.

The man Achelous called Meri smiled at her, his arm in a neat, dark sling that matched his shirt. Her silly heart stuttered in her chest.

"My lady," he said. "It seemed a fine night for a visit to your rose garden."

She took him in, noting that his hair did not move in the wind, that he balanced too easily with his right knee upraised and his left leg dangling. "Then why aren't you actually here?"

His grin grew wider. "Because I have a day or two left before I'm well enough to get out of bed. Achelous didn't mention he'd talked to you about how we cast our avatars."

"Does he usually tell you every detail of the conversations he has with others?" She strolled forward, more relaxed now that she knew she could not hurt him. With the barest lift of her wings, she joined him on the wall, staring out toward the flickering lights of the town in the distance.

"If he did, it sounds like you would not approve."

"It's not my place to approve or not. That's between you and him." She turned her head to look down at him as she spread her wings and let the breeze ruffle her feathers. "But to have to report every movement to another. It is not...a good feeling."

His smile faded like the stars at morning. "It is not. And I would never make him do such a thing. I too have had my every moment accounted for, my every movement noted. It is suffocating. And I hated not just every minute of it, but the people who forced it on me."

She crouched, bringing herself to his level so she could see his face better, her wings arched high above them. "Did they trap you in a place you could not leave as well?"

He nodded, his gaze steady on her.

"Was it...jail?"

His eyebrows lifted, then laughter rolled from him in a joyous, melodious wave of sound. She caught her breath. She'd never heard a human laugh so easily and so fully. As if his entire body was part of his mirth. She found herself grinning at him, wishing he was truly there.

It's better he's not, she reminded herself. *You can't endanger him and the Aello can't hurt him.* Because she could never see this man hurt. She knew that with her whole heart and whatever soul a creature like her had. He was freedom and joy, and as long as he was in the world, she believed it truly could be better than the bad things in it.

"I have been briefly deprived of my liberty by...the authorities in the past. But I have never been imprisoned for long."

"Your father never forced you to do his bidding?"

All levity dropped from him like a discarded coat. His eyes narrowed. "Is that what the Archmagus does to you?"

She looked away, unable to meet the anger in his gaze. It made her feel that this man understood her. And that made her vulnerable. Made her ache for...what, she could not say. She only knew that she didn't want to have to part from him. Her wish to see the world, her plan to leave forever...for the first time, she was not alone in it.

"The Archmagus. Who is he to you?"

Father. Teacher. Jailer.

"A powerful man," she said. "With many rules. You are breaking them when you come here, and he is not to be crossed."

"I'm dangerous when I'm crossed too," he said softly, and the menace in his voice made her glance at him again. His mouth was tight, his hands fisted.

"Were you dangerous to those who kept you trapped as well? The ones you say you hated?"

His lip lifted at one corner, and he huffed out a breath. "No. That was...different."

"How?" She was curious now. Something told her this was a sensitive topic, but she wanted to know more of him. His secrets. She wanted to know everything.

He was silent for so long she thought maybe he would not answer. She waited in the heavy, sweet musk and lifted her face to the sky, silently counting the stars. She didn't mind the silence now that he was in it with her. It wrapped them in a fragile companionship like nothing she'd felt before.

"It was my mother," he said.

She turned to him, stunned, heart racing. He met her gaze, but there was shame in the rueful twist of his lips. *Are all families like mine then? Do humans force their children down paths they decree, willing or not?* "She locked you up?"

"She had expectations for me. I tried to meet them for years. But I grew...restless. Despondent. She didn't understand. I'm not like her. It's always been about duty for her. Responsibility."

"To the family," Iris said softly. Gentle surprise flashed across his face, and he nodded.

"Yes. My father died before I ever knew him. I was trained from birth to one day take over the family business she inherited upon his death."

"But you do not wish to."

For the first time he looked away. She saw him swallow before he said in a low voice. "It doesn't matter now."

"Why?"

"I was very foolish once upon a time and I hurt her, very badly. Hurt myself as well. After that, I understood how much I had to learn. Many things changed, and I changed with them."

For the first time, she wished she could hold someone. There was something lonely about the way he squared his shoulders. He was like a wild thing, untouchable and fierce, yet she longed to take his hand and settle her head against his shoulder.

"You're sorry for what happened."

He took a deep breath. "Very much so, yes."

"Because you love her." How she envied him. He'd known love his whole life.

"Because she loves me." He met her gaze and his lips parted to show a glimmer of a sad smile. "Despite everything. And I took her for granted. Achelous made me see that."

"She is a good mother then." *Nothing like the only one I've known.* "And he is a good friend."

He hesitated, and she felt it down to her bones. There was something here he was not sure he wanted her to know. *Tell me. We are the same, you and I. Let us know each other.*

He grinned ruefully and shook his head, as if he heard her. Then held her gaze and said in a gentle voice, "He's more than that."

"More than a friend?"

"Yes."

She thought on what she knew of humans. Then it came to her. *More than friends indeed.* A new-found heat rose within her, touched her in secret places. She dropped her gaze. "Oh. That."

"Yes. That. But he's more even."

"How is that possible?"

"Because he is special. There is a bond between us you cannot imagine." He said it as if he needed her to hear every word. "He saved my life. Saves it still. Every day."

Heat and cold chased each other across her skin. She twisted her fingers together, trying to rationalize the jealousy that stabbed her in the gut. Not just for Meri's devotion to Achelous. But what that meant about how Achelous must feel for him.

I want what they have.

No. That wasn't right.

She wanted them to feel for her what they felt for each other. She wanted it from them both.

What was wrong with her? Two strangers had come into her house, uninvited, and instead of fear, they'd brought her a glimpse of a world she was desperate to see. To think of seeing it with them. To want them. She must be mad. This must be madness.

It could lead to nothing good. Not when she had no chance of escape now. They would move on to wherever they were headed next, and she would be left here, alone and trapped, never to see them again.

"Iris, look at me."

It was best if she put an end to this. She should never have encouraged it. Never have tried to know him. Asked questions when she had no right to answers. Already she had a hint of the pain losing them would bring. She could not risk more.

"You should go back now," she said. "Achelous must be wondering where you are."

"No, he isn't. He always knows how to find me when he's finished with his duties. Iris. I need you to look at me."

She raised her head and was surprised to see how close he was. He'd leaned forward, his hand on the wall between them, his legs dangling on either side.

"There is a bond here too. I feel it, goddess," he said, his voice low and sweet inside her, like wine warming her belly. No one had ever called her by anything but her name, but the word he used felt truer to her than that even.

"I...why do you call me that?"

He ignored her question, a strange light in his eyes. "I felt it when I met you that first time. I tried to follow you on that path, and I cursed myself for a fool that I let you go."

"No one can step on my path but me," she said, her voice soft and bewildered. He was saying things that wrapped her heart in warmth she'd never felt before. And her mouth, oh her mouth was sweet as plums and dates. Truth always tasted like fine wine and fruit on her tongue.

"I know that now. But I have a second chance and, Iris, I do not intend to waste it."

"I don't understand," she said. "We can be nothing to each other. You are a thief passing through. I'm a monster in a cage."

"You are a beauty in a tower, and no one has ever managed to keep one of those locked away for long."

He was telling the truth. Her breath laboured to free itself from a tightening chest. She looked down at their hands, side by side on a rough stone wall. She watched as he deliberately placed his over hers, watched as it faded to a shimmering outline she could not feel, but wished she could. Still, the sight sobered her—filled her with a painful resolve.

"It's no use. We cannot even touch without my killing you."

"I don't need to touch you," he said. "Do I want to? The Old Gods know I would love nothing more. But what I *need* is to be with you. To talk with you. There are things I want to know. Things I want to say. Experiences I want to share with you. I want to be your friend, Iris."

"Friend." She closed her eyes and took a shaky breath. "Friend?" She opened them and rose to her feet, spreading her wings for balance. He looked up at her, a supplicant at her feet that she could not give the simplest of benedictions.

"You already have one, remember? And I? I have never had need of friends."

There was such softness in his gaze. "You, Iris, have need of them most of all."

It was the splash of cold water she needed. The reminder she held onto like a drowning man holding onto driftwood. "No," she said, her voice sharp and breaking. "Don't do that." She fluttered down off the wall, ignoring him as he jumped down next to her.

"Iris—"

She strode away from him. "The last thing I want is another person in my life telling me what I need."

"You are right, I shouldn't have said that. What I meant was—"

She reached her doors and turned to face him with an upturned hand. She could hear the Aello stirring, hear a guard approaching. To take her tray, most likely.

"They are coming. You have to go now."

The light from the bedroom illuminated the fleeting frustration on his face. "Don't push me away, Iris, you know I'm right."

"I hope you and Achelous are happy together," she replied. "Don't come back, because if the Archmagus ever realises you've been here, he'll hunt you both down. And then he'll hunt your families."

She saw the shock cross his face before he narrowed his eyes at her. "Is that how he keeps you in line? With violence and chains?"

Her breath caught as the image of the Stone rose in her mind. She just managed to choke out, "If you have a care for me, or Achelous, or your mother, Meri, forget you ever met me."

She slammed the doors in his face.

It should not have surprised her, perhaps, that Achelous was in her room less than an hour later, but it did. He knelt at the side of her bed as she sat up.

"Iris—"

"No, Achelous. I'll tell you what I told Meri. You must leave and never come back."

His broad face was so much easier to read than Meri's. Every emotion he felt flitted across its strong planes. His openness called to her in the same way Meri's joy did.

"I'm sorry for whatever he has done to offend you. He often speaks and acts impulsively, but it is because he wishes to help."

"Achelous..."

"Please, Iris, allow me to speak with you on our behalf."

She frowned. "Our?"

He nodded, and the kindness in his eyes almost brought the tears she rarely cried to her own. "When he spoke to you of friendship, he was not offering for himself alone."

Friendship. Of course.

She sat on the edge of the bed. "I don't want that from either of you, Achelous. And he did not offend me. I asked him to leave because you endanger yourselves by coming here, and for what?"

"Because this is no place for you," his words were low, firm and the rumble of them settled in her bones like a heavy portent. "And we do not wish to leave you in it."

"He cannot take me out of here, so why does it matter to Meri if I stay?"

"Why does it matter to *us*?" he replied, his gaze searching hers. "Meri is not alone in caring about what happens to you." He stood with a sigh, looking down on her. "He may have seen you first. But—Iris, I would know now. Do you feel for us as we feel for you?"

He could not mean what she so desperately wanted him to mean.

"I...would see neither of you hurt. It is why I'm telling you to go."

"That is not all I meant, Iris."

She would not give herself false hope.

"What do you mean then, Achelous? Because I know nothing of what either of you do, but I know enough to presume the life of a thief and his companion is one of constantly moving, constantly searching for new treasures to steal, while evading those you have robbed. So these visits and these *feelings* you both have for me…they are temporary, are they not?"

The fleeting regret that crossed his face was enough of an answer. She lay down again and turned her back to him, the weight of that revelation crushing her into the bed. "Go, Achelous."

"I will go," he said in a soft rumble. "Because you wish it. Not because I do. And Iris…I will not speak for Meri. I will speak for myself. My feelings are not temporary. And when something threatens the people I care about, I will find a way to protect them, whatever it takes."

"You can't care about me," she said to the wall across from her. "Those I've lived with for my entire life don't care about me. Why would you be any different?"

"Sometimes people are blind to who we are. That doesn't mean others will be. I see your heart. You are a gift, like the traveller's star. Once it appears, we follow it always. We trust it to lead us where we wish to go. Trust your instincts, Iris. Meri and I have learned over the years, our instincts are never wrong. And they tell us you are meant to do more than stay in this tower."

"Then *your* instincts are wrong," she replied. "Because now the Archmagus knows I was false, he will never let his guard down enough for me to find a way out. And trust is something I have never known. Do not ask it of me."

"Iris—"

"No. There is nothing more to be said."

After he left, coldness ached within her. She wrapped her wings around herself as she imagined the arms of a lover would.

5

A Gift

The next day, she put Meri and Achelous from her mind and went in search of Eleni. Perhaps she could reason with her. Make her understand, the way Meri had seemed to. His mother had loved him even after his mistakes. Eleni was mother to the flock. She'd raised Iris with her own hatchlings. It could not be so impossible for her to see things from Iris' point of view.

But when she found her, she knew she was wrong. That there would be no swaying her.

Because she was directing several of the Aello in the huge stone kitchen as they dismembered the Forager's remains with gloved claws and preserved it in fluids for the Archmagus' use and study. Directing them by pointing the axe in her hands.

"What are you doing?" she said, horror making her voice loud.

Eleni glanced at her. "Why are you not in your room?"

Iris could not take her eyes off the axe. She hugged her wings to herself reflexively.

"Why do you have that?"

Eleni looked down at the blade in her hand as if surprised to find it there. Then she turned to Iris. "It is the only thing that can cleave the body."

For the first time in her life, Iris found it difficult to breathe the very air. She grabbed the rough wood of the door jamb for support.

"You...you're using that thing. In front of me. After everything." She searched Eleni's face. "You truly don't care for me at all, do you?"

Eleni sighed. "One has nothing to do with the other. You should not have left your room. Then you would not have seen."

Her words speared Iris to her heart. "What does it matter, Eleni, when you plan to show it to me again once the Archmagus returns? Or have you decided you will not help him this time?"

The other Aello had slowed their work to better observe the confrontation. The silence stretched for some time, broken only by the clatter of jars and the splash of liquids. A faint smell of decay and burning grew stronger every second Iris spent with her eyes locked on Eleni.

Finally, the matriarch spoke. "The Archmagus is our protector. He has my assistance in all things. As he should have yours."

This time, Iris was braced for the inevitable. She let the numbness take her as she replied, "Not in this. *Never* in this. And you are without soul or conscience to expect it of me."

Eleni shrugged. "We Aello are not given to delusion. Pretending we do not know what he will do is delusion. That will gain you nothing. Perhaps it would be better for your soul and your conscience if you finally made your peace with what is expected of you instead." Turning her back in dismissal, she gave more orders as Iris stumbled out of the room, her claws beading blood in her palms.

She sat on the bench on her balcony, a book open and forgotten in her lap as she stared at the rose bushes along the wall. As the Archmagus' return drew close, she could not stop thinking of what father would do and say when she saw him.

There had been punishments before. Days of fasting. Weeks without books. But she knew what awaited after the worst infractions.

Last year, a retrieval had gone wrong, leaving a guard at her feet, writhing and screaming as he died from her touch. Eyes, mouth, nose, hair—all of it bleeding. The stink of him losing his bladder and bowels. The iron scent of his death.

The horror of what she'd done had sent her flying on her rainbow path, determined never to return to the Citadel. Until a terrible, wrenching pull deep in her guts dragged her back through the open door of her bedroom, where the Archmagus waited, his face twisted in anger.

It's the Stone for you. And Eleni will not intervene. The care you thought she showed you. The dinners and concern. It was all a lie.

A shudder ran through her, and a scalding tear escaped, dripping onto her hand.

"Now that just won't do."

When she looked up to see Achelous filling the doorway to her room, Meri leaning on him with one hand while the other hung in a sling off his shoulder, she could not name the feeling that flashed under her skin, warming her entire body.

"Can you not, just once, say hello like a normal person?" Achelous asked, looking down at Meri with an annoyed glance.

But Meri kept his eyes on her. "Who has made you cry?"

She wiped at the tear and put her book aside. She had never cried in front of anyone. She wouldn't start now. "I told you not to come back. Why are you both here again?"

"I had to see you." Meri paused. "I could not stop thinking of what you said. Ash agreed with me that we had to return."

She looked away, sighing. "There's nothing either of you can do."

"Tell me why you're crying, goddess."

Her heart kicked in her chest at the word.

"You may as well answer," Achelous said with a grunt. "He won't stop pestering you until you do."

"Don't bother to lie. I'm quite good at lies and can discern them easily," Meri added, his lips twitching in a brief smile even as he focused his penetrating gaze on her.

"Oh, what does it matter? You're both there and I'm here and soon—" She stopped, her breath hitching as she thought of the Stone.

"Yes, soon?" Meri's voice was soft, commanding. "Tell me."

She closed her eyes. "The Archmagus will return home and I will be punished. For failing in my duties. For my disloyalty."

Achelous cursed and Meri asked in the same voice, "And what form will that punishment take, Iris? What will he do to you?"

All she could get out was, "The Stone." She jumped up from the bench and strode over to the bushes, unwilling to let them see her fear.

She was ashamed that after all these years, a tear had fallen when strangers could see. But she knew what the Stone was now, and it was hard to contain her anxiety. Her anguish.

"There's nothing you can do," she said to the white roses in front of her. "They've increased security and the Archmagus will return any day now. If you're discovered, he'll cast wards, and I'll never see either of you again."

"And would that bother you? Never seeing us again?"

She hugged herself and let out a shaky breath. "You're the first humans I've spoken to, besides the Archmagus. I've lived my entire life without seeing any of you."

Except for the guard last year. Except for the man I killed.

"Yes, but is that what you want? To never meet anyone outside of the Citadel again?"

She tilted her head back to stare at the evening sky, white tufts of clouds floating past in a sky so pale, it was almost grey.

"Iris," came the gentle voice of Achelous. "What do you want?"

"You know," she said, "no one's ever asked me that. What I want."

She closed her eyes, the wind blowing the sweet scent of roses past her as she stood in silence. *Should I tell them?*

She sighed and opened her eyes.

It was so hard to trust.

Trust your instincts.

"I want to leave. I make plans. I save things I will need. But I know it's a lie. And not just because he'll never free me. Who would have me? Where would I go?"

"We would." Meri's voice vibrated with an intensity that fired her blood. "Anywhere. Everywhere."

She turned and looked at them, studying their faces. For the first time, Meri didn't wear a smile and Achelous had a glint in his eye that reminded her of his earlier anger.

She could hear the uncertainty in her own voice as she said, "Don't say things you don't mean. I know there's nothing out there for me."

"There's nothing in here for you either, except pain and isolation. Am I right?" Meri asked, fingers flexing on Achelous's arm.

"Eleni would say I have a purpose. A family."

"Is that what you call a bickering nest of monsters that threatens its own with violence?"

She flinched, stung. "If they're monsters, what does that make me?"

He didn't hesitate. "Their prisoner."

"I'm—"

"Don't," Achelous broke in, his voice harsh. "You're no monster. By the Gods, I've spoken to you but twice and even I know that. How is it you don't?"

"Because I've killed people!" she cried. "And I've done things. Things I'm not proud of. Things that—hurt others."

"And yet none of it was your choice, was it?" Meri replied, his lips a straight, grim line. "Iris, we must all live with our decisions, but those that are forced on us are never truly ours. And what is this purpose you speak of? To guard a building filled with another man's treasures?"

"I told you," she said with a wave of her hand, "I should have reported you that night, yes, but I'm no guard."

"What do you do then?"

She paused, part of her not convinced she should share such secrets with strangers.

"I assist the Archmagus."

"With what?"

She shrugged, avoiding their gazes. "Whatever he needs."

Achelous grunted. Meri sighed. "Alright. You don't know us. I understand. You have a right to your secrets. But, Iris, no one has the right to take your freedom. To hurt you."

Anger seared through her. "You think I don't know that? He doesn't force me to do this. I agreed to it."

"Because you believe things about yourself that aren't true."

"You're right about one thing," she said, gripping her elbows tight, "I don't know you. And I think it best things stay that way."

"You'd rather cling to lies than consider another path?"

"It's not that simple. What right do you have to come here and criticize me when you are a thief and a liar yourself? All you've brought me is trouble. Why should I trust your opinion on matters you know nothing about?"

She saw the fury that flashed across his usually serene face. It was a startling change, one that warned her this man had depths he would not show easily.

"Because," he ground out, "I know what it is to be lied to by those you love. What it is to be held prisoner by duty and fear when all you wish is the open sky and a life of your own.

"Perhaps I don't deserve your trust, but I swear to you, Ash and I don't wish to hurt you. We want to give you a chance at your own life. Your own choices. I look at you and I see myself, years ago. I have no regrets now. I want the same for you."

His gaze travelled over her, and she felt it like the almost forgotten caress of fingers. "You are...extraordinary, Iris. I had no idea you were in this Citadel. But if I had known, I would have climbed these walls to you the night we first met."

She knew he meant every word he said. But there was something else in his face. Something cautious and hidden.

"That's not all, is it?" she asked, taking a step toward them.

Achelous threw a quick look at Meri as the thief glanced away from her.

"Since the moment I saved you, you've kept something from me. Something you recognized about me. What do you know?"

She watched his throat bob as he swallowed. "I can't know for sure, Iris. Since I found you here, we've been trying. Achelous consulted with more than one magus about our suspicions these last few days. But...we could be wrong."

"Meri," Achelous said, his deep voice a growled warning.

Meri met his gaze, eyes narrowed. "What would you have me do? If I'm wrong, she could lose her life trying to escape. If I'm wrong, he's strong enough to stop her."

"And if we are right?" the larger man said. "We decided it was worth the risk. She has no other options. But quickly, now." His voice turned grim, and he lifted his head, sniffing as if scenting something. "We haven't much time left."

"We have a gift for you," Meri said. He reached into the pouch around his waist and laid a thin, silver bracelet on her bench.

Iris gasped. "You're here? In the flesh? But...the Aello will sense you—"

Achelous waved an impatient hand. "That's not the point. We want you to have this. I spent the last few days making it. If they come to take you to the Stone again, be sure to have it on. Only you can see it, so do not fear they will take it from you."

"Why?"

He glanced at Meri and the thief answered her, "Because then we will know what the Archmagus has done. Once we know the truth of it, we can help you escape."

Magick crackled through her veins, awareness shivering every cell in her body awake.

Father. He's returned early.

She stared at Meri, her throat closing on the words, but it didn't matter. He saw her panic on her face.

"Ask him. Ask the Archmagus," Meri said. "If he cares for you at all, as you believe, it's past time you've heard the truth. Ask him where he found you. Ask him when."

"In a sea cave. Many years ago." She frowned. "He never kept it secret that I was abandoned."

Meri flung his hands up. "You see, Ash!"

"We're probably right," the other said, and relief was in his eyes as he looked at her.

"Enough of your games," Iris demanded, striding over to them. "Tell me!"

She heard movement throughout the castle. The Aello rising to greet their master. Dread clutched her with cold fingers, as much for what approached as what Meri would say next.

"You care for this Archmagus. I don't think he deserves your love. But if there's a chance he's not what I believe, I have no right to accuse him. So, you put that bracelet on, and you ask him a question, Iris."

"What question?"

"Ask him what happened to your parents."

She shook her head, bewildered. "He never knew my parents."

"If I'm right, he did."

Achelous held tight to Meri. "He's too close. There's no more time."

"If I'm right, he killed them," Meri said, and they both vanished, taking her breath with them.

6

FRUIT AND WINE

The bracelet was a circlet of linked flowers—irises. She snapped it closed over her wrist and stood looking at its lustre. When she drew her fingers over it, the warmth of Meri's body was still on it. It thrummed slightly at her, most likely with the magick that kept it hidden.

She was sitting on her bench, waiting, when Belen and the others came to get her. She let them march her down into the lowest levels of the Citadel without a word of protest. They closed her into father's vast study and left her alone. She sank down on a stool, her gaze going unerringly to the small door at the far end of the room, a chill chasing across her skin as she imagined the cold space beyond.

When the Archmagus came in, he was still in his traveling clothes. His sturdy boots echoed on the slate floor as he went to his desk, and there were dust stains on his open overcoat. He tugged his gloves off as he leaned against the desk and slapped them onto a sheaf of papers that collapsed into a heap under the assault. He didn't meet her eyes at first, choosing to comb his fingers through his hair and beard and scrub them over his face.

She waited. She could not speak when her throat had closed in on itself and all the words in her head belonged to Meri.

He faced her, pinning her to where she sat with his dark gaze.

"Explain yourself," he said. His tone was ice and without inflection. She clenched her hands so hard, her nails pricked at her palms.

She licked her lips, opened them to reply—and could not answer.

If I'm right, he killed them.

"You know how important this trip was," he continued in the face of her silence, "and I was forced to cut it short because you defied the guards for a thief. A thief!"

She licked her lips.

I could keep up the pretense. Get on my knees and beg his forgiveness. If I show enough contrition, he might believe me long enough for me to find a way out.

Except he wouldn't care. She had broken the rules. The Archmagus was a man of ruthless discipline; he never backed down from his decisions. She had always known what ultimate punishments awaited her if she ever betrayed his loyalty.

And she was tired of doing his bidding. Tired of wearing meekness like too tight clothes.

"Not only did he escape, he will no doubt try his luck again because you prevented the Aello from doing their job. I have endured your fits of rebellion long enough, Iris. This time, you've—"

"Did you kill my parents?"

Her voice brought his to a halt. She kept her gaze on his inscrutable face as the moments ticked away.

"Did you really find me in a cave, father? Or did you take me from my family? My real family?"

He flinched. "You know how I feel about that word."

"Yes, but why? You're the only father I know. You've fed me, clothed me, kept me safe. Kept others safe from me. So, why can't I call you that? Does it bother you to be reminded I once had one?"

He pushed himself off the desk with one hand.

She stood, feeling her skin flush hot and cold.

Why won't he answer me?

"Did you kill my parents?"

"What has made you ask this?" he said, eyes narrowed. "Did you find something—" He stopped speaking and she seized on his silence.

"What? What do you think I found?"

"You are impertinent."

"Do you know what happened to my parents? Did you know them?"

Her voice boomed through the room, the sound amplifying on itself. Father stiffened as he looked her over.

"No," he said.

And there it was. The taste of bitterness on her tongue. Like aloe and crushed leaves.

"Liar," she whispered, her heart seizing in her chest. "By the Gods. You've lied to me. You've lied to me *my entire life.*"

She saw a tremor travel up the arm that rested on the desk. He shifted under her stare, bringing his arms across his chest.

"That's enough," he said in a quiet voice. "You know how I feel about hysterics."

"Hysterics?" she breathed, as wrath scorched every feeling in her body, leaving numbness in its wake. "You dare to charge me with that when you kept the truth of my life from me? When you imprisoned me here for years on a false pretext?"

"I did what I had to," he bit out. "I've told you the truth. You are a danger to the world, and the world is a danger to you."

"You've hidden something. Meri knew it the moment he saw me."

He gritted his teeth. "Who is this Meri? Is he the thief?" His eyes widened. "Have you fallen under the thrall of a man you don't even know? One that tried to steal from us? Haven't I raised you better than that?"

She flung her hands up. "Raised me? Is that what you call teaching me to bury my thoughts and emotions, forcing me to stay here, and to fear anything or anyone outside these walls? To hate my own skin?"

He drew in a breath and surprise swept across his face. "I never taught you to hate yourself."

"You never taught me to love myself!"

"Has this stranger—this *man*—has he spoken to you of love?" His voice was full of scorn. "Is that why you turn against me this way? Has he been here before?"

She stared at him, aghast, her rage at boiling point. "How shallow and pliable you think me. But then again, you duped me easily for years."

"I would know if this man has seduced you."

Inside, she knew there was a kernel of truth to his accusations, but she would never give him the satisfaction of it. Not now. Not when she needed answers and he refused to give them. He would claim nothing more from her. He owed far more than he could ever repay.

"Know this, *father*. We were strangers to each other. Yet he saw the truth so swiftly, I know now why you didn't wish me to leave the Citadel. You feared how easily someone would tear apart your lies."

"I feared your death!"

She stumbled backward, unprepared to hear him raise his voice for the first time. His breathing was harsh, his mouth tight. Shock rippled through her as she saw panic in his eyes.

"You made me think I was the dangerous one," she whispered.

"You are." He closed his eyes and sank onto the desk, both hands holding the edge as his head lowered. "Because you don't know your own power. And I cannot teach you. Something happened to you, before I found you, and you have never had the knowledge—the control. And those that could teach you—those who might know what went wrong—they are gone now. I've searched for many years and found no one. They've all been killed."

"Killed?" She took a step toward him. "These people—my people—were murdered?"

"There was a war. They lost. And the Diviners and their war-beasts hunted those that remained and wiped them out."

"But why?" Her voice broke. "Who are the Diviners? Who were my people? Why would the Diviners kill them?"

"Because they were a threat to the new power the Diviners had brought into this world." He met her gaze, took a deep breath and spoke. "Because they were Gods."

Silence settled around them as her mind stuttered to a halt. "Gods?"

He nodded, slow and tired. "At least one of your parents was an old God, Iris. And ever since the war ended, any old God or demi-god the Diviners have come across, they've killed without hesitation. So, you see, I hid you because I had to. Because I could not let you die. There's enough death on my head. I will not have yours as well."

Fruit and wine sat on her tongue, and she fell back onto the stool, stunned.

"I only knew your mother," the Archmagus said quietly. "I saw her come out of the ocean with you and crawl into a cave. I left her there after she died and took you as far away as I could. If the Diviners had wounded her, as I suspected, I knew they would come to finish her off. If I'd left you there, they would have killed you too. At first, I thought maybe you weren't her child. You were like any human baby. But the wings..."

"My wings," she repeated dully. "When they grew out, I stopped being able to touch others. Why was that?"

"I'm not sure. Perhaps you are simply too powerful."

She slid her hand along the soft glimmer pooled in her lap as she shielded herself with her wings, as though they could hold back the pain of his words.

"Who was my mother?"

"I think she was a sea nymph. A child of a sea god. I have no way of knowing who your father was."

"Why were you there? How were you even at the ocean to find me?"

He hesitated.

"Please," she said. "If you have a care for me, as you claim, let there be no more lies between us. I will know."

He nodded. "I've always known you could sense the truth. It's why I tried not to discuss your past."

Her vision grew blurry. "So you could fool me better."

"So I wouldn't have to explain what I knew. Who you were." He heaved a breath. "What I'd done."

"Why were you there?" she repeated.

"There was a battle nearby, between the Diviners and the Breach Gods, and the old Gods and their armies. One of the last great ones. I was picking through the battle-field, looking for magicks that might be useful."

"Is that how you collected all these..." she waved her hand around.

"Some of it, yes. I was only a mage then. Magick was all I cared for, all I burned for. The war made it possible to see and learn so much. I did whatever I had to do to gain more knowledge and see the greatest of magicks, first-hand." His gaze was steady on her face now. "That's why I joined the Diviners' army and fought wherever they sent me."

It was too much. All the truths overwhelmed her, made her mouth fill with nauseating sweetness. She low-ered her head into her hands with a moan, prickles racing up and down her skin.

"You—you helped them? For how long?"

"The war lasted seven years, and I fought for five. I stopped the day I found you. I'm not proud of what I did, but magick is everything to me, Iris. I had to be near it."

She rose to her feet, wishing she could rinse the agoniz-ing taste of truth out of her mouth. "I know. I've travelled the rainbow path for you, retrieved so many treasures. All this time, I thought it brought us closer. That we had a bond. That deep down you must love me a little to let me be part of your quest, your life's work. But what you loved was your magick."

He said nothing; his black eyes took her in without a trace of emotion. It made her shiver with rage.

"Or am I wrong? Did you love me a little because I was magick? Because I was your greatest treasure, locked in here with all the others, for you and you alone? Capable of bringing things to you that no one else could find, or bear to touch? Did you love me because I was the ultimate prize, something no other Archmagus would ever have?"

His lips moved, but she held up her hand. "Don't. I've had enough."

She couldn't hear him say 'no' and have it be the truth. And she couldn't bear for the answer to be 'yes' either. All she wanted was to leave. Get away.

"Please, let me go to my room."

For long moments they stared at each other, he impassively, she with so much pain and anger the air thickened with it. Then he turned from her and went behind his desk.

By the time she reached the door, she could hear the scratch of pen against paper.

Once inside her room, she didn't hesitate. She packed the few things she owned: her money and books; a change of clothing; her woven cloak, the one she wore when she went to dark places where her light would bring dangerous attention. She stared at the beautiful bracelet on her arm, thinking of the men who had given it to her for an agonizing second. They had been right. About all of it. But she could not think of that now. She had to move quickly. She had no food, and she would need more money.

Father had plenty. He kept it in his study—along with the quill that controlled the tattooed chains on her wrists. She had felt it in there this time. Felt the tightening of the chains on her.

He'd moved it from the Treasury the moment she'd used her time with the hatchlings to search for it down there, and she'd not sensed it since. But tonight, it was near. She would bide her time, wait until the Citadel went to sleep, find the quill, and free herself.

But when she crept downstairs hours later and pushed the study door open, something tiny flew out of the darkness and bit into her chest. By the time she'd plucked the dart from her skin, she had already begun to fall, her eyes drifting closed before she hit the floor.

7

THE TRAVELLER'S STAR

She woke naked in the cold, chained to the Stone. Her wings were spread on either side of her, on the huge slab of granite, held down by straps. They cast refracted light in the glow of the candles around her. The same light gilded the bracelet on her left arm.

Eleni stood to her right near a table with cloth and healing tinctures. She did not meet Iris's eyes as father strode around the Stone, checking the chains on her arms and legs. It was no use struggling, she knew. The Stone leached all magick into itself, an effect that would last for hours after contact. Her touch had no power. She closed her eyes, tears leaking from them.

It was a trap. He knew I would come looking. He always knows.

"How can you do this to me?" she whispered. "After all the lies, after all you've done, you would force me to suffer like this again?"

He stood over her, a crease between his eyes. "They will grow back, and the clipping of them doesn't hurt. I would never let anything hurt you. I can't risk you leaving. You're too important to me to let you be betrayed or killed by the first person who guesses what you are."

Her eyes widened as she stared at him incredulously. "Is that what you believe? That because you use an axe that severs without pain, you've never hurt me? You hurt me every moment you kept me trapped here. *You took my wings.*"

He sighed. "I give you everything you need. You've only read books and perched on walls. The world out-side—the Diviners—would swallow you whole."

"How would you know when you've never let me go anywhere without chains?"

He leaned closer, his sigh puffing against her face. "Because I know *you*, Iris. I know your soft heart and your dreaming mind. You're the last of your kind, and too young to be trusted with your own power. If you stay with me, I'll find a way to help you wield it. But you'll never learn what you're capable of if you leave."

"I'll never learn anything but what you wish me to if I stay. And that's all you care about, isn't it?"

"Archmagus, please," Eleni said, handing the ancient axe to him. "It is cruel to prolong this."

The Archmagus glanced at her, sighed and nodded before stepping away.

Iris pulled at her bonds, unable to stop herself despite the knowledge she could not escape.

"I hate you," she gasped at Eleni.

"This is for the best, child," the matriarch replied. "You can't see all he's done for you."

Iris swung her head to look at the Archmagus. "I'm sorry I ever let desperation make me call you father. You're a beast who uses everyone around you. I will never help you again."

He drew a gloved hand over her soft, springy hair. "You'll eventually understand that this is for your own good. And if you don't." He shrugged, his fingers flexing on the axe. "All children hate their parents at one time or another. It comes with the territory."

The door opened. "Oh dear," Meri said, "am I interrupting a family spat?"

The Archmagus froze in the act of raising the axe and Eleni cursed.

Iris stared at Meri, who closed the door and leaned back against it, settling the arm in the sling against his chest.

"So, this is the Stone you were afraid of. Doesn't look like much to me."

"Meri, what are you doing?"

"Helping a friend," he replied, and there was an odd energy to his voice. "Remember what you said before. How you weren't forced to stay here? That you agreed to it? This Stone is the confirmation of everything Achelous and I believed might be the truth. I am sorry for the deception, but I could not risk him tricking our plan out of you with this Stone. And these chambers were too secure for me to enter before. I had to wait until something I tied myself to entered them again."

The bracelet. Iris inhaled in shock and stared down at her hand. It glowed back at her, bright as her wings.

"*You,*" the Archmagus breathed. "You're not supposed to be here. You're supposed to be in Ingmar."

Meri raised his eyebrows. "Have we met?"

Iris saw the shocked horror on the Archmagus' face, glanced from him to Meri and all at once, she understood.

The mirror. His greatest enemy. It was Meri. He saw Meri.

"You're a Merchant Lord?" she gasped.

He inclined his head to her, an amused tilt to one corner of his lips. "Only when I'm not biding my time in a cell, or scaling walls to rob a magus of his treasures, of course." He swept her a quick bow. "But my friends know me as Meri."

Dread filled her. She knew what the Archmagus did to those who threatened him.

With no warning, the Archmagus flung the axe. Meri shifted and it embedded itself in the door next to his head.

"Have you lost your mind?" Iris cried. "Go! Save yourself!"

"Get out of my Citadel," the Archmagus said in a voice like cold thunder.

Meri ignored him. "You believed things about yourself that weren't true. Now you know it was all lies, he's brought you here to take your power. Because if it wasn't the truth, he wouldn't need to do this to you."

With a one down beat of her speckled wings, Eleni flew at Meri. He ducked out of the way as she slammed her claws into the door. For a moment, she hung there, cawing, struggling to pull her talons free.

"Get up," Meri said.

"I can't!" Iris tugged at her chains. "The Stone takes my magick, my strength."

The Archmagus began muttering an incantation under his breath.

Meri took a step toward Iris, his eyes narrowed, his mouth grim. "I've heard of many artefacts, stolen even more, but I've never heard of a stone that could do that to anyone, much less a demi-god, because *that*, Iris, is what I sensed you were the moment I saw you."

He turned a furious gaze on the Archmagus. "I *have* heard of a stone that makes anyone who touches it believe what they're told. The Suggestion Stone used to sit in the temple of Prometheus. It was a creation of Dolos, the father of lies and trickery. And you can stop your muttering, old man. None of your spells will work."

Eleni got her claws free, spun and slashed at Meri's head. He side-stepped her and she crashed to the ground, momentarily stunned.

"That must hurt," Meri said, his eyes still on the Archmagus.

The Archmagus hissed in anger.

"Get up, Iris," Meri said, his tone low and direct. She saw her own fury in his eyes and so much compassion her heart swelled in her chest. "You're all you need. You always have been. You know the truth now. Have the strength to live by it. When you are ready, come find us."

He must have used the Rebound incantation, because the next thing Iris knew, Meri had gone and Eleni was pulling the axe from the door and stalking back, her feathers on end, her wings high.

"See how he cares for you?" she ground out. "He leaves you with nothing but words. You would abandon your family for a man like that?"

A Suggestion Stone. What if it has all been suggestions? He tied me here every time I rebelled. He would lecture me and I would relent and do whatever he wanted. Until the day lecturing me wasn't enough.

On her wrist, the light of the bracelet faded away, until her arm was bare again.

The Archmagus took the axe from Eleni, and she retreated out of the way.

He took my wings that one time. But they grew back. If the Stone takes all magick, why did it come back?

He turned to her.

Because I'm free. I've always been free. But I have to choose it. I have to fight for it.

The Archmagus raised the blade above his head. Iris looked up at him and said, "No."

He stumbled backward, the axe falling from his hands. "Iris," he said, his voice a warning.

She glared at him, grabbed at the chains that crossed her palms and imagined them breaking into shards, imagined her straps springing loose.

Her restraints crumbled to dust.

She sat up and spread her shining wings, forcing the Archmagus to narrow his eyes. He took another step back, his face tight, his nostrils flared. "Don't do something you'll regret."

She leaned down and plucked the axe from the floor, hefted it in her hands as she rose to her feet above them both. A startled squawk escaped Eleni's lips.

"Can you guess what I won't regret?"

There was no warning, no sound when he left her alone with Eleni.

"Apparently, you can."

She arched her eyebrows at Eleni. "See how he leaves you with nothing but words?"

The crown of feathers on Eleni's head lay flat. She stilled, her eyes bright and wide. "Kill me, if you must. But everything I did, I did to protect you."

"Kill you?" Iris stared at her. "You think I let myself be kept here, trapped in my room with barely a kind word from him because I wished any of you harm?"

She breathed out, sorrow and resentment flowing through her as she raised her arm and slammed the axe into the Stone beneath her feet. It split around the blade, which sank into it like a spoon into broth. She felt the magick leak out of the Stone like water from a sieve until it was nothing but cracked granite. Power sizzled up her arms like a lightning strike. Her entire body, her head, her chest, the tips of her clawed toes, even the never touched space between her legs, jolted with energy and heat.

At that moment, the axe in her hands changed. The humble wooden handle shrank, becoming metallic shorter and easier to grasp. Delicately worked patterns of swirls and bands etched themselves into it. The blade of the axe blunted, becoming a square block, the whole of it golden as the sun. The other side of the axe's blade narrowed to a thick, pointed end.

This was no axe, she realised, but a hammer. Of course, it was magick, like all other artefacts. But she'd never encountered an inanimate object that transformed like this.

Nor one that filled her with such a sense of strength and *wholeness*. She had broken the Stone that had held her down with it. Now, there was nothing trapping her here.

Breathing hard, she stroked upward and hovered. "Achelous was right. I don't belong here. If you both believe I could kill so easily...if you both fear me like this...I was always in the wrong place."

Eleni tilted her head as she gave Iris a slow blink. "You don't know that man. You don't know what lies outside these walls. You don't even know yourself."

"You still think this is about him?" Iris said, her voice hard. "He's not the one who helped imprison me, Eleni. He's not the reason I'm leaving. I know what lies are *within* these walls. And I understand myself enough to know I want no further part in them."

The Archmagus did not appear when she reduced the locked door to dust and left the Stone room. Somehow, she knew she would not see him again. The fear she had felt for so long was his to keep.

The tattoos on her wrist faded like smoke as she pocketed his money. She hesitated only a moment before selecting several small artefacts as well, including the carefully wrapped Enmity mirror. They went into a charmed sack with what had once been an axe, but was now a little hammer that rumbled in her hands like Achelous' voice. The deep vibration of power was like nothing she'd ever felt before.

Whatever happened after today, she had no intention of leaving it with him to be used on her, or anyone else, ever again.

After she'd taken what she wanted from his study, she went to her room to dress and collect her things. She could have walked out of the front door now she knew nothing could hold her. But she wanted to do what had been denied her for too long.

She heard the Aello gather at her door long before she looked up. Belen stepped into her room alone, while the others stood silently in the corridor outside, eyes unblinking.

"I won't see her, Belen. She knows what she did."

He opened his mouth, gathered his thoughts before speaking. "She understands. Do you?"

"No. And I never will."

He sighed. "That's fair, I suppose."

"Did you know? Did everyone?"

"No," he said, his voice firm. "She kept it from us too. She was wrong, Iris. But we make decisions in the moment, and we live with the consequences. We don't look back. It's our way."

She stopped moving, clutching her hands tight on her bag before releasing a breath.

"If you leave, the Ciceros will have another name to keep for us all."

"The chicks will miss you," someone added. "No one else reads to them."

"For good reason. Waste of time," an elder said, before they squawked, irritated as they were jostled and jabbed into silence by several others.

She straightened and looked at them all, memorizing their faces one by one. Heart hurting for the faces that weren't there. The faces she would be a Cicero for.

"I'll miss you too. But I must do this."

Belen's chest swelled and deflated. "It's time."

She nodded. "It's time."

For long moments, they were silent.

"Well then," said an elder. "Chicks leave the nest. It's only natural. Nothing to see here."

They flew off as one leaving Belen as the lone sentinel in her doorway.

"Take care of them," Iris said.

Belen spread his wings and followed the flock.

Iris strode through the doors to her balcony and stopped to breathe in her roses one last time. Elation rose within her, floating upward like a feather on the wind.

I'm here. I'm really doing it.

The freedom she'd hungered for flooded every cell of her body with lightness.

What do you want?

She could do anything now. Go anywhere. See the world without fear of a leash yanking her back to high walls and cold stone.

Clutching her bag, she drifted up onto the wall. The air was sharp and cold as metal in her lungs, and she saw far and wide. In the distance, the town sparkled a hundred golden lights at her. Above her, a star glimmered brighter than all the others. The traveller's star.

Is that what you want?

It was Meri's voice in her head now. She knew so little of him—of them both. She could not forget the Archmagus had seen Meri in his mirror. He was his greatest enemy. If she went to them—a thief with magick and his half-human companion—there was no guarantee she wouldn't be in danger. No guarantee the truth of who they were wouldn't leave revolting sweetness in her mouth.

Meri was his greatest enemy because he recognized the lies the Archmagus had told me.

And he and Ash had not kept the truth from her. Instead, they had spent days searching for a way to help her escape. They had offered her their friendship and a place with them. That said something important about them too.

And what they had, the tension that arced between them like an electric charge... She wanted to be part of that.

Needed to be part of it.

For the briefest moment, she thought on the Archmagus and his warnings. On Eleni and the Aello. On the Forager she'd killed. Who knew what terrible things came next—what awaited her in a world she knew so little about?

It matters not what comes next. I'm already everything I need. I have been this entire time.

There was no fear at all in her now. No Stone.

She smiled to herself.

She knew what she wanted.

The rainbow path glimmered to life, flowing straight as an arrow toward the town in the distance.

Come find us.

Iris lifted her dazzling wings under the night stars and launched herself at the heavens.

ABOUT THE AUTHOR

R.S.A. Garcia is a Nebula and Sturgeon Award winning writer of speculative fiction. She is also the winner of the Machine Intelligence Foundation for Rights and Ethics' 2023 Media Award, and a Locus, Ignyte and Eugie Foster Award finalist.

Her Amazon Bestselling science fiction mystery, *Lex Talionis*, received a starred review from Publishers Weekly and the Silver Medal for Best Scifi/Fantasy/Horror Ebook from the Independent Publishers Awards (2015).

She has published short fiction in venues such as *Clarkesworld Magazine*, *Uncanny Magazine*, *Escape Pod*, *Strange Horizons*, *The Sunday Morning Transport*, and *Internazionale Magazine*.

Her stories have been long-listed for the British Science Fiction Awards, translated into several languages, and included in a number of anthologies, including the critically acclaimed *The Best of World SF*, *The Best Science Fiction of the Year*, *The Year's Best Fantasy*, and *The Apex Book of World SF*.

The first book in her sci-fantasy duology, beginning with *The Nightward*, was published in October 2024 by Harper Voyager US.

She lives in Trinidad and Tobago with an extended family and too many cats.

www.ingramcontent.com/pod-product-compliance
Lightning Source LLC
Chambersburg PA
CBHW070518200726
48293CB00007B/2592